W9-BGP-405

Ebbie & Flo

Irene Kelly

April 2005
Rachel + Jason,
Happy
(fishing)
(+ reading)!

Irene Kelly

A Smith and Kraus Book for Kids

For Jeffrey, Derek and Lucy

Special thanks to Marisa and Eric

Text and Illustration Copyright ©1998 by Irene Kelly
All rights reserved

Ebbie & Flo

No part of this publication may be reproduced in whole or in part, or stored in a retrieval system,
or transmitted in any form or by any means, electronic, mechanical, photocopying, recording,
or otherwise, without written permission of the publisher.

For information regarding permission, write to:
Smith and Kraus
PO Box 127, Lyme, NH 03768

A Smith and Kraus Book for Kids
Published by Smith and Kraus, Inc.

Library of Congress Cataloging-in-Publication Data
Kelly, Irene.
Ebbie & Flo / by Irene Kelly.
p. cm.
Summary: Flo is a daredevil salmon while her brother Ebbie is a more cautious fish, but during their journey
downriver to the sea, they come to appreciate the differences in their personalities.
ISBN 1-57525-115-9
[1. Salmon—Fiction. 2. Brothers and sisters—Fiction.] I. Title
PZ7.K29615Eb   1997
[E]—dc21   97-39852
CIP
AC

Manufactured in the United States of America
Art Direction by Julia Hill, Freedom Hill Design

First Edition: May 1998
10   9   8   7   6   5   4   3   2   1

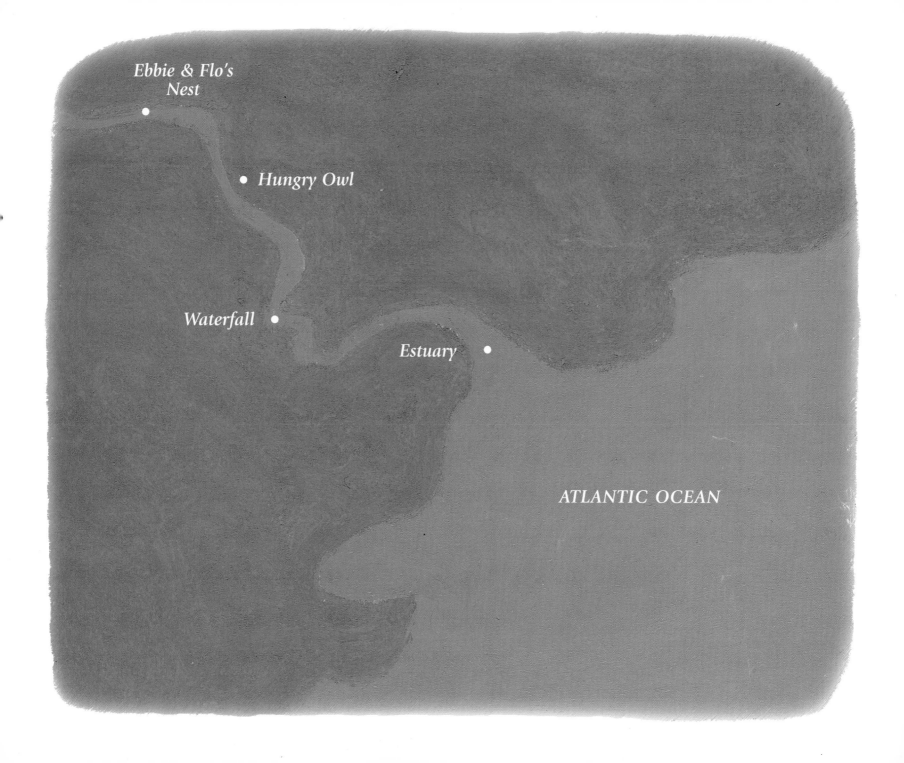

$\mathcal{D}$EEP IN THE WOODS, in a quiet stream,
a mother salmon laid her eggs.
"What beautiful eggs," the father said.

The parents covered the eggs with pebbles
to keep them safe and snug until they hatched.
Then they said good-bye.

The two fish were beginning their long journey
back to the ocean, far, far away.

There were lots of eggs in that nest
but this story is about only two of them.
They were brother and sister
and their names were Ebbie and Flo.

They were as close as close can be.

The little salmon grew inside their eggs for fourteen weeks
until one spring day when everything changed.

"We've hatched!" Flo shouted. "We're free!
WE'RE SWIMMING!"

"This is going to be even tougher than I expected,"
Ebbie muttered as the strong current
swept him downstream.

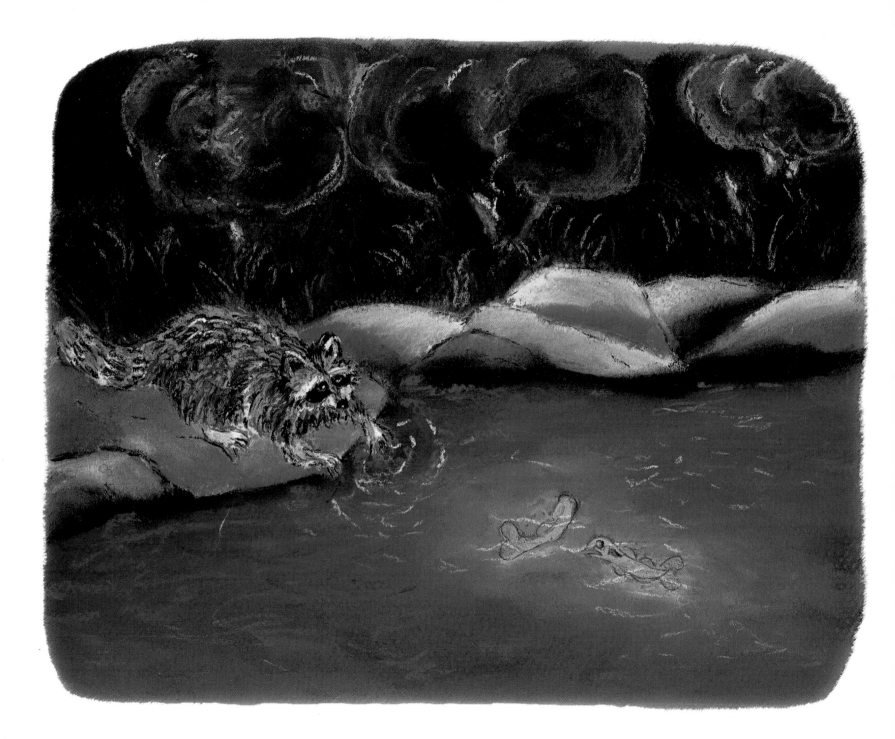

Flo was brave. She laughed at hungry owls.

Ebbie didn't.

Flo was athletic. She could fly over boulders.

Ebbie couldn't.

Flo was daring.
She nibbled the worm
at the end
of a fishing hook.

Ebbie fainted.

One night Flo let the river's current
pull her tail-first around a bend
and into the unknown.

"Be careful!" Ebbie warned.
"Don't worry so much," Flo replied.

Just then, Flo was swept over a giant waterfall!
Ebbie tried to turn back but he couldn't fight
the strong pull of the falls.

Over he went.

"That was great!" Flo yelled.
"I can't wait to go to the ocean!"

Ebbie shivered. "Do we have to?"

"Of course we have to go to the ocean," Flo declared.
"We're salmon and that's what salmon do."
She swam away as fast as she could,
deep into the cool water.

Ebbie sighed and slowly followed.

Ebbie and Flo traveled down the river for a whole year until they finally arrived at the estuary, where the fresh river water meets the salty sea. Here they rested while their bodies adjusted to the saltwater. Ebbie liked the estuary. The water was calm and the coves were perfect for hiding.

But they were salmon and this wasn't the end of their journey.
"We are ready to swim in the ocean," Flo announced one morning.
Ebbie didn't want to leave but he knew that Flo was right so they
left for the ocean as soon as the moon came up.

Flo was fearless, even in the ocean. She loved meeting the mysterious creatures living there.

Ebbie wasn't so sure.

One day Ebbie saw an enormous shadow
moving towards them.
"What's that?" he wondered anxiously.

"I think it's a whale," Flo said. "Let's go see."
And she swam straight toward the shadow.

"Be careful!" Ebbie called.
"Don't worry so much," Flo replied.

Suddenly, Flo was staring into the eye of a killer whale!
He opened his enormous mouth and lunged at the little fish.
"HELLLLLLLPP!" Flo cried as she vanished into the ocean with
the giant mammal chasing after her.

Ebbie didn't know what to do.
Flo needed his help! Now *he* had to be brave.

Ebbie raced off in search of his sister.

He followed the low humming of the whale's voice
far out into the sea.

He was lonely and very scared
but he didn't give up.
Then he saw the shadow.

It was them! The whale was swimming
in slow circles around Flo, ready to attack.
Ebbie had to save her.
He swam faster than he ever had before
until he was in front of the killer whale.
Ebbie turned and faced the creature and shouted,
"LEAVE HER ALONE!"

That made the whale laugh.

Then Ebbie shouted,
"YOU BIG BLUBBERY BULLY!"

That made the whale furious.

He opened his huge mouth and rushed towards Ebbie.
In a flash, Ebbie torpedoed to the bottom of the sea.
The whale spun about, wondering where the spunky
little salmon had gone.

Hiding deep in the ocean, Ebbie found his sister.
"Flo!" Ebbie shouted, "Are you all right?"
"You saved me!" Flo said. "When you shouted
at the whale, I escaped. You really are brave!"

"I guess I am," Ebbie replied proudly.
The two fish stared at each other in
silence for a moment.

"Soon it will be time to swim back up the river
 to where we were born," Flo said.
"Do you think we can actually leap UP the waterfalls?"

"Of course," Ebbie said, smiling at Flo.
"We're salmon and that's what salmon do."

And off they went.

FISH FACTS

There are many types of salmon. Atlantic salmon like Ebbie and Flo spend much of their teenage and adult life in the Atlantic Ocean.

Female Atlantic salmon lay their eggs in freshwater nests called redds. Every redd contains several hundred eggs which the mother fish covers with gravel. After three or four months the baby salmon, called fry, hatch. Each is about one inch long and has a large yolk sac attached to its body, providing the perfect nourishment for the young fish. This allows the fry to focus on hiding from predators without needing to search for food.

After six weeks the yolk sacs are used up and the fry must find their own food. They eat tiny plankton and insect larvae as they grow and develop in the territory they will claim as home for the next one to three years. During this period the fish begin to change in appearance, developing dark patches on their bodies which camouflage them from the many hungry animals and birds hunting them. Now the salmon are called parr and are considered a fine meal by many: owls, herons, hawks, kingfishers, raccoons, bears, otters, larger fish, and people.

Before migration begins, the salmon become more silvery in appearance and are referred to as smolt. They begin their journey to the ocean, arriving at the estuary within two months. This water has some salt in it and the fish will spend a short time here allowing their bodies to adjust to the new salty environment.

Gradually the salmon swim far out to sea, feasting on herring and anchovies and growing quickly. Soon they are too big to be consumed by wading and diving birds like herons and kingfishers but become prey for sea lions, whales and seals. The salmon may spend four years in the sea before they return to the river.

Eventually the fish leave the ocean and begin the difficult journey upriver to the gravel beds where they were born. They identify their birth river by the chemical smell of the water, rocks, soil and plants. The salmon gather in large schools at the mouth of the river to begin their travels together. As soon as the first heavy rain makes the river rise, they start their return trip. The salmon stop eating once they begin to swim upriver. They survive on the reserves of fat they have stored up while living in the sea. The fish jump and push through the water, fighting the river's strong currents and leaping up waterfalls. They can cover many hundreds of miles before reaching their destination.

When the salmon finally reach their birthplace, they mate and lay eggs, completing the life cycle. The tired and hungry adult salmon drift slowly back to the sea. Atlantic salmon may repeat this journey several times during their lifetime.